Movie Novelization

New Girl in Town

Movie Novelization

Better together

by Marilyn Easton

SCHOLASTIC INC.

No part of this publication may be reproduced, or stored in a retrieval system, or transmitted in any form or by any means, electronic, mechanical, photocopying, recording, or otherwise, without written permission of the publisher. For information regarding permission, write to Scholastic Inc., Attention: Permissions Department, 557 Broadway, New York, NY 10012.

ISBN 978-0-545-54762-8

LEGO, the LEGO logo, and the Brick and Knob configurations are trademarks of the LEGO Group. © 2013 The LEGO Group. Produced by Scholastic Inc. under license from the LEGO Group.
Published by Scholastic Inc. SCHOLASTIC and associated logos are trademarks and/or registered trademarks of Scholastic Inc.

12 11 10 9 8 7 6 5 4 3 2 1   13 14 15 16 17 18/0

Book design by Becky James and Angela Jun
Printed in the U.S.A.   40
First printing, January 2013

Table of Contents

Chapter 1: Meet Olivia

It was the day before the Heartlake City World Petacular. Butterflies were fluttering around the park as everyone worked on the final preparations for the big day. There was going to be a horse competition, a pet adoption, and a surprise musical performance!

Olivia was busy helping her aunt Sophie, Heartlake City's veterinarian, set up some tables and animal cages for the pet adoption. Olivia had just moved to the neighborhood, and Aunt Sophie thought being a part of the Petacular would be a great way for her to make friends.

"Olivia, thank you for helping me set up for the pet adoptions tomorrow. With so many people coming to the World Petacular, I think we can find homes for lots of the animals at my clinic," said Aunt Sophie.

"Of course! Is there anything else I can do?" Olivia asked.

Suddenly, a woman approached Olivia and Aunt Sophie. She was holding a cute brown puppy in her arms.

"Excuse me," she said, handing the dog to Olivia. "I just can't keep this puppy anymore. She chews on everything and won't behave." The puppy looked up at Olivia with big brown eyes.

"Aw, this little girl? She just needs to be trained." Olivia smiled at the pup. "And bathed," she added, wrinkling her nose.

"I think she needs a better home, but I can't provide her with that. Her name's Scarlet, by the

Olivia meets Scarlet

way. Good luck," said the woman. She turned and walked away without looking back.

"Looks like we've got our first puppy for the pet adoptions," Olivia said to Aunt Sophie.

Scarlet licked Olivia's face as if to say she was ready for a new home.

"Olivia, maybe you should take Scarlet for a walk to the horse-riding ring," Aunt Sophie suggested.

"Why?" Olivia asked.

"There's someone I want you to meet. Her name is Mia. She's a champion horse rider. Since you've been in Heartlake City two weeks now, I figured you'd like to start making friends," Aunt Sophie said.

"Yeah . . . but not *arranged* friends," Olivia said quietly.

"Aw, don't worry, Olivia. Mia is one of the friendliest girls I've ever met. You're going to have

Aunt Sophie's advice

fun, I promise. Oh and make sure to keep a firm hold of Scarlet's leash," Aunt Sophie warned.

"Of course I will, Aunt Sophie," Olivia replied.

But Scarlet had other ideas. She spotted a

 5

butterfly and ran right out of Olivia's hands!

"Scarlet! Oh, no! Come back!" Olivia called as she chased after the energetic puppy.

"Be careful, Olivia!" said Aunt Sophie.

Olivia hurried after Scarlet. She was one quick pup! All of the sudden, Olivia bumped right into a boy. *Wham!* The boy's model airplane fell to the ground.

The runaway puppy

"Whoa, sorry!" Olivia called as she tried to catch up with Scarlet.

"It's okay. I couldn't get it to fly even before you ran it over," he said.

Olivia glanced back. "Close the needle valve half a turn, then restart," she suggested.

"I doubt that'll work," said the boy to himself. But when he did as Olivia said, the plane flew! He tried to thank Olivia, but she was already too far away.

Meanwhile, the mayor was holding a town meeting to make sure all of the preparations were on schedule for the World Petacular. He was standing in front of a beautifully designed sign with the Petacular logo on it.

"The World Petacular is the biggest event that Heartlake City has ever hosted. We have horse competitions, a dog show, pet adoptions, grooming, pet care, and more. This will surely put our town on the map!" the mayor announced.

Suddenly, Scarlet burst through the sign—leaving a huge hole right in the middle!

The crowd was in total shock. So was the mayor.

"Oh, no!" Olivia cried. But she couldn't stop. She kept chasing after Scarlet.

As Olivia looked ahead, she could see a girl painting a big banner. The girl, Emma, needed to add just a few more paw prints. Olivia tried to warn her that Scarlet was off her leash, but it was too late. Scarlet splashed paint all over the nearly finished banner!

"Scarlet, bad dog!" Olivia said. "Sorry!" she called back to the girl as she ran after Scarlet.

A few paces ahead, Stephanie, a baker with a passion for planning, had just finished icing her final cupcake. She had been a little behind

Emma finishes her painting.

schedule but was making up time nicely. That was, until Scarlet arrived!

"Look out!" Olivia called. But Scarlet had jumped all over the cupcakes before Stephanie

Stephanie's cupcakes

had a chance to move them out of the way. "So sorry!" Olivia cried. "She's, uh, in training!"

With all of the trouble Scarlet was causing, Olivia would never make friends in Heartlake City!

It looked like Scarlet's next stop was going to be the café. Inside, an aspiring singer named Andrea had just finished singing a beautiful song, and the customers were cheering.

"Thanks, everyone," Andrea said to the crowd. "You can hear more from me tomorrow at the World Petacular."

"Fantastic," a customer said. "Now, how about my hamburger?"

Claire, the owner of the café, was used to Andrea's impromptu performances. "Order up, Andrea. I've been ringing the bell for five minutes," she called.

Andrea frowned. "I wonder if other singers started this way," she said to herself.

She picked up the order, carefully balancing three plates of food on one arm and a tray of drinks on the other.

At that moment, Scarlet burst into the café and ran circles around Andrea's feet. The little pup startled

Andrea and made her lose her balance.

"*Whoaaaaaaa!*" shouted Andrea as her plates and drinks flew up into the air.

Olivia arrived just in time to see everything come crashing down on the floor. She'd pretty much ruined her chances of making any friends now.

Andrea's balancing act

Chapter 2: The Chase

While Olivia continued to chase Scarlet through Heartlake City, Mia was practicing jumps with her horse, Bella, in the horse-riding ring. Mia and Bella needed to be at their best for the jumping contest tomorrow. Mia loved competing, but this year the competition was really tough.

"Nice one, Bella. That one had 'gold medal' written all over it," Mia said encouragingly after Bella had landed a perfect jump.

Just then, Lacy and her white horse, Gingersnap, trotted over. Lacy was Mia's main competition.

"I wouldn't be so sure, Mia. Gingersnap is a champion," Lacy said.

"May the best horse and rider win," Mia replied confidently. She wasn't going to let the competition bring her down.

"Thanks. *We* will," Lacy sneered as she rode off.

Mia and Bella with Lacy and Gingersnap

Bark-bark-bark-bark!

Scarlet was running toward Mia and Bella. Oh, no! Scarlet darted underneath Bella. The horse was so scared that she reared back on her hind legs.

"Whoa, Bella! Whoa!" Mia said nervously.

Mia carefully dismounted as the puppy ran

Scarlet startles Bella

circles around Bella's hooves. But before she could get a firm grip on Bella's reins, the horse ran away!

A moment later, Olivia breathlessly ran into the horse-riding ring. "Now where did that dog go?" Olivia said to herself as she turned to look behind her. She stepped forward—and bumped right into Mia! Both girls fell to the ground.

"Sorry, my horse got spooked by this puppy running by," Mia said as she brushed herself off.

"Oh, no. Are you Mia?"

"Yeah . . . Are you Olivia?"

"Yeah. And this mess is all my fault," Olivia explained.

Scarlet was finally too tired to run anymore. She plopped down at the side of the ring. Olivia took the opportunity to scoop her up.

Just when Olivia thought things couldn't get any worse, she looked up to see Emma, Stephanie, and Andrea all heading toward her. The girls didn't look happy, and she couldn't blame them.

"I worked for three hours on that banner and that puppy wrecked it in three seconds!" Emma said.

"My horse ran off and we're supposed to compete tomorrow!" Mia said angrily.

"I'm already super busy with rehearsals and my

17

work at the café. I definitely don't have time to clean up after that puppy!" Andrea added.

Stephanie whistled for everyone to stop. "Everyone, relax! Look, we're all upset. But let's give Olivia a chance to explain," she said. "Not that it'll help," she added under her breath.

"I don't have time. I have to go find my horse right away," Mia exclaimed.

Olivia meets Stephanie, Mia, Emma, and Andrea

"Mia, we can take my car and find Bella in a minute. I know it's hard for you, but people come first," said Stephanie, "then animals."

Mia frowned and folded her arms. "Fine."

"Do you all know each other?" Olivia asked.

"Sort of. I'm Stephanie. That's Mia, and you're Emma, aren't you?" Stephanie asked.

"Yes," replied Emma.

"I'm sure you all know my name. I'm the official singer for the World Petacular," Andrea said. The other girls gave one another confused looks. "I'm Andrea," she added, feeling a bit embarrassed.

"Oh, I know you!" Emma said.

"Really?" Andrea asked with excitement. Finally, someone recognized her!

"Yeah! You gave me the wrong order last time I was at the café," said Emma.

"Oh, right. That sounds like me," replied Andrea.

"It's nice to meet you all," Olivia said. "I just moved here two weeks ago. My aunt warned me about the puppy—and the leash—but I didn't listen. I'm really sorry and . . ." Olivia trailed off.

Suddenly, the mayor came running over in a panic. "Stephanie!" he called. "Stephanie!"

"Mr. Mayor—" Stephanie began.

"What on earth is happening here? The World Petacular has to go perfectly. All of the people are coming to our city, and these fairgrounds are a disaster! Who is responsible for that runaway puppy?" the mayor demanded. He was upset.

Olivia opened her mouth to admit it was all

Heartlake City's mayor

her fault, but Stephanie jumped in before she could speak.

"It doesn't matter, sir. Placing blame won't fix anything. Don't worry, everything's under control . . . almost," Stephanie said.

The mayor was still not satisfied. "But how? What—"

"I'm going to assemble a team to fix everything. I've handled situations far worse than this," Stephanie assured the mayor.

"Really?" Emma asked sincerely. "Like what?"

"*Shhh,*" whispered Stephanie, winking.

"Stephanie, I'm counting on you. I'll go reassure our sponsors and special guests. Unlike me, they're very nervous," the mayor said. He hurried away.

Once he was out of sight, Andrea turned to Stephanie. "Stephanie, who is this team that's going to fix everything?" she asked.

"Yeah, they sound amazing!" said Emma.

"It's Team You-and-You-and-You-and-You-and-Me," Stephanie said, pointing to all the girls and then herself.

"*Us?* Do all *that*? By tomorrow?" Mia said in shock.

"Yes, we just need a place to work and get organized," Stephanie said confidently.

The team

"There's a tree house near my house," Olivia suggested.

"That's perfect! Who's in?" Stephanie said.

All the girls cheered except for Mia. She wasn't interested.

"Okay. You can count me out," Mia said. She

Stephanie makes peace

turned to Stephanie. "Can we go find Bella now?"

Stephanie nodded and gave the girls a reassuring look. She'd talk to Mia. If this team was going to work, they definitely needed her to be on board.

Chapter 3: The Team

The girls drove around Heartlake City looking for Bella, but they weren't having any luck. Mia had almost given up hope when she spotted Bella at the edge of the forest, hiding behind a tree.

"There she is!" Mia cheered.

Stephanie pulled over. As Mia got a closer look at Bella, she noticed her horse was limping.

"Oh, no," Mia gasped. "Hurry! We have to call the vet!"

A few minutes later, Aunt Sophie arrived with Olivia, Emma, and Andrea. Aunt Sophie looked concerned. "Easy, girl," she said. "We better get her

Mia and Stephanie search for Bella

to the clinic. Her leg needs an X-ray."

"An X-ray? Is it really that bad?" Olivia asked. She looked worried.

"We might not be able to compete," Mia said sadly.

As they helped Bella into the horse trailer, Lacy rode by on Gingersnap.

"What happened?" Lacy asked.

"Bella's hurt. We're taking her to the clinic," Mia explained.

"I'm sorry to hear that," Lacy said with a hint of a smile. She turned and trotted off.

Olivia turned to Mia. "Mia, I'm so, so sorry," Olivia apologized. She felt terrible.

✳✳✳

Back at the vet clinic, Aunt Sophie reviewed the X-ray of Bella's leg. Mia looked on nervously.

"Good news. Nothing's broken," Aunt Sophie said.

Bella's X-ray

"Thank goodness! Does this mean she can compete?" asked Mia.

"It's too soon to tell. Let's see what the morning brings. Here, help me with this ice pack," said Aunt Sophie.

Mia helped Sophie apply the ice pack. Then they bandaged Bella and walked her to a stall.

"So, about Olivia . . ." Aunt Sophie began.

"Do we have to talk about her?" Mia asked sharply.

"I still think you two could be good friends," said Aunt Sophie

"Thanks, but I'm not really getting the friendship vibe," replied Mia.

"Everyone makes mistakes. And everyone deserves a second chance," Aunt Sophie added.

Mia thought about it for a moment, and then nodded. Maybe she had been too hard on Olivia after all.

Later that afternoon, Andrea and Stephanie headed back to the café to bake new cupcakes for the Petacular. Olivia and Emma went to check out the tree house. Olivia brought along Scarlet for the trip.

The tree house was a cool, woodsy space with green grass and shrubs.

"This place is great, Olivia! It just needs a few finishing touches," Emma said. "It would make such a great hangout for everyone," she added.

"Yeah. Everyone except Mia." Olivia sighed.

"I don't think she'll ever talk to me again."

"Just give her time. She'll come around," Emma said reassuringly.

"I hope so. All right, I'm going to start training Scarlet," Olivia said.

"That's perfect. I'll put the finishing touches on my new banner," replied Emma.

 30

Emma and Scarlet

Olivia climbed down the ladder. "It's training time," she told Scarlet.

Scarlet let out a little whine, but then she perked up when she saw the delicious treats Olivia was holding.

"Scarlet, sit. Sit. Sit . . ." Olivia commanded. But Scarlet jumped up and snatched the treat right out of her hand!

"Scarlet, no!" Olivia scolded. She grabbed

Training time!

another treat and kept working. Every time Olivia told Scarlet a command, Scarlet just gave her a puzzled look.

"Scarlet, if you don't start behaving, no one is going to want to adopt you. Don't you want a good home?" Olivia said. "Somewhere in there you have to know that you've caused a lot of trouble. Even though part of it is my fault, a lot of it is yours. Mia may not be able to compete now, and she's worked so hard. You owe me."

Scarlet seemed to understand what Olivia was saying. The little pup was ready to learn at last. She worked really hard, and eventually Olivia had Scarlet sitting, staying, rolling over, and heeling!

After all her training, Scarlet was ready for her final test.

"Now, sit," Olivia said. Scarlet obeyed.

"Roll over." Scarlet rolled over.

Then Olivia took a few steps backward.

"Stay," Olivia commanded the puppy. Scarlet stayed.

"Heel," commanded Olivia. Scarlet heeled and Olivia gave her a treat.

"Good girl!" cheered Olivia.

"Not bad," a voice said. It was Mia! She had been watching the whole time.

New friends

"Thanks. My aunt Sophie taught me how to train dogs," Olivia answered.

"She thinks highly of you," said Mia.

"Does that seem crazy?" Olivia asked. "Especially after all the trouble I've caused?"

"Not as crazy as it seemed earlier today. Do you or Emma need any more help?" Mia asked.

Olivia smiled. Maybe she could make some friends after all. "You know what, I could use some help giving Scarlet a fresh look! Let's call the other girls for their expert opinions."

Soon Scarlet was surrounded by hair and nail clippers, and a pile of doggie accessories.

The experts get to work

Emma, Olivia, and Mia were just about to get started when Stephanie and Andrea arrived to help.

"Makeover time!" Emma cheered.

Emma gave Scarlet a haircut while Andrea and Olivia clipped her nails. Stephanie and Mia chose between sparkly dog collars, bright bows, sunglasses, and even a golden crown!

Finally, the girls decided on Scarlet's perfect look—a pink collar and a bow.

"Girls, I think we found just the right look for her," said Emma. Then she turned to the puppy, "Don't you agree, Scarlet?"

Scarlet barked happily.

Scarlet's new look

Chapter 4: Saving the Day

The next morning, Mia ran over to the vet clinic. She needed to make sure Bella was feeling better. But when she got to the stable, Bella wasn't there.

"Sophie! Bella's missing!" Mia cried.

Then Mia turned and saw Aunt Sophie riding Bella. Bella was trotting around as if her injury yesterday had never happened! Aunt Sophie dismounted and handed Mia the reins.

"She's all better," Aunt Sophie said with a smile.

Mia mounted Bella and trotted over to the fairgrounds. She couldn't wait to tell her friends about Bella's recovery. It was amazing!

Bella's all better!

"Morning," Mia called to her new friends.

"Mia! Bella's okay?" Olivia asked.

"She's more than okay; she's ready to bring home the gold!" said Mia.

"Everything is working out perfectly," said Emma.

But Emma had spoken too soon. Suddenly, there was a huge crash. The pet adoption stage had collapsed!

"Oh, no!" Stephanie cried.

"That did *not* just happen," said Andrea.

Stephanie saw a construction worker heading toward the stage. She ran over to him.

"What happened?" Stephanie asked the worker.

"I don't know. Something must have gone wrong with one of the support beams," he explained.

"Can you rebuild it in time for the Petacular?" Stephanie asked.

"Sorry, I don't have all my workers here today," he replied, scratching his head. "With so few

Teamwork time!

people, we'll never get it done on time."

"What about us? I'm pretty good with the hammer, and I can draw up some blueprints," Olivia offered.

"You can use my sketchpad," Emma suggested.

Stephanie pitches in

"Come on, let's hurry . . . we only have a few hours!" said Stephanie, putting her arms around the girls.

Olivia's blueprints

The friends got to work right away. They
assisted the two workers with hammering and
carrying pieces of the stage. Olivia oversaw the
whole operation. She looked at her blueprints and
gave the crew clear directions. Everyone pitched
in. Even Bella helped with some of the heavy
lifting!

As the last board was hammered into place,
the girls took a step back and glanced at the stage.

It was finished—and it looked even better than before!

Just then, the mayor appeared. He had heard about the stage catastrophe. "Stephanie, you did an amazing job," he said.

"Thanks, Mr. Mayor. But I had a lot of help from my friends," Stephanie explained.

"I didn't think we could get everything done," said Andrea in disbelief.

"Me neither," Mia added.

Celebrating a job well done

"It only worked because we had the right team," Stephanie explained.

"If we saved the World Petacular, I wonder what else we can do!" Olivia said as the girls all looked at one another. They really had accomplished something great.

The mayor glanced at his watch. "It's time to start the festivities," he said.

"I have to go. I've got a little surprise," called Stephanie, hurrying off.

"You're leaving? Now?" Andrea asked.

"What surprise?" Emma asked. But before she could get an answer, the microphone onstage turned on. The World Petacular was about to begin!

Chapter 5: The World Petacular

"Ladies and gentlemen, it's my great privilege to welcome you all to Heartlake City. I declare the World Petacular open!" the mayor announced to the huge crowd.

As the mayor finished speaking, there was a noise in the sky. Everyone looked up as an airplane flew overhead pulling a WELCOME TO THE WORLD PETACULAR banner behind it.

"There's my banner!" Emma said proudly.

"And look who's flying the plane!" said Olivia with surprise.

It was Stephanie, with a boy seated behind her.

Stephanie flies by

They both waved. Olivia recognized the boy—
she had helped him fix his toy plane after Scarlet
bumped into him! But before she had a chance to
ask Emma about him, she glanced at her watch.
The pet adoptions were about to start!

Olivia rushed over to the adoption stage.
There were many families lined along the runway,
eager to find a new pet.

Backstage, Olivia began prepping Scarlet.

"Okay, Scarlet, it's showtime!" Olivia said as she fixed Scarlet's bow. "And you better *behave*," she added.

Aunt Sophie stood at the microphone. "And next up for adoption is . . . Scarlet! A lovable mixed breed, Scarlet enjoys playing and going for walks. She is fully trained."

Showtime for Scarlet

Olivia and Scarlet walked out on stage. Scarlet held her head high. She was proud of her new look—and the tricks she had learned.

"Scarlet, sit," Olivia said.

Scarlet sat and looked at Olivia for the next command.

"Scarlet, heel," said Olivia.

Scarlet walked at Olivia's heels. The puppy had done a perfect job. She was definitely going to get adopted now!

✳ ✳ ✳

Over at the horse-riding ring, it was time for the competition. Mia and Bella were getting ready for their final jump. Emma, Stephanie, Olivia, and Andrea were cheering them on from the stands.

"I didn't know you knew how to fly," Olivia said to Stephanie as they waited for Mia and Bella.

"I'm still learning, but it's really cool," Stephanie replied.

"Who was that boy?" Olivia asked, trying to not seem too interested.

"Jacob, my flying partner. His dad owns the aviation school. He's sort of annoying though," Stephanie answered.

"Oh, you really think so?" Olivia asked.

"Yeah, why?" Stephanie replied.

"No reason," Olivia said and blushed a little.

"Look, there's Mia and Bella!" Andrea cheered.

The girls watched anxiously as Mia skillfully rode Bella over the horse jumps. But on the last

Watching Mia and Bella's big moment

one, Bella's hoof caught the bar, and it fell. The friends all cringed.

"Oh, no," Olivia said. The girls looked at one another. They felt so bad for Mia.

The announcer's voice came over the loudspeaker. "Oh, that was a tough jump for Bella. Looks like that's going to knock Mia out of gold medal contention. And that means our gold medalist is . . . Lacy and Gingersnap! And coming

Mia's good sportsmanship

in second place is Mia and Bella!"

Mia waved to the crowd. She was proud to get second place—after all, she had worked really hard.

Mia walked over to Lacy and shook her hand. "Nice job, Lacy. Congrats," she said with a big smile.

"Aren't you mad that you didn't win?" Lacy asked.

Mia looked off to the sidelines where Olivia, Stephanie, Emma, and Andrea were.

"I did win something: new friends," she replied.

"Great job, Mia," Stephanie called from the stands.

"You're going to win the next one," Emma said with a smile.

"I'll have to catch up with you guys later. I need to go see how Scarlet is doing with her adoption," Olivia said. She waved good-bye to everyone.

✳ ✳ ✳

As Olivia approached the adoption center she saw Scarlet's previous owner talking to Aunt Sophie.

"I can't believe the difference in Scarlet. You did such a great job. Could I possibly re-adopt her?" the woman asked.

Olivia and Aunt Sophie exchanged concerned looks.

"Uh, I guess. I mean . . . it's just that we've been through so much," said Olivia nervously, "and . . . I was sort of hoping to—"

"Actually, she's already been adopted," Aunt Sophie explained to the woman.

Olivia was shocked. *Who adopted Scarlet?* she wondered.

A new home for Scarlet

"Oh, what a pity. Well, good-bye, Scarlet," the woman said, giving Scarlet a little pat on the head. She waved good-bye to Olivia and Aunt Sophie, and walked away.

"Who adopted Scarlet?" Olivia asked.

Aunt Sophie placed Scarlet in Olivia's arms. "Think of her as my gift to you," said Aunt Sophie, smiling.

"But my parents—" Olivia said in shock.

"I'm sure I can work things out with them," Aunt Sophie said. She gave Olivia a hug, and Scarlet licked both of their faces.

Olivia hugged Scarlet. She couldn't believe the little puppy was really hers! She went to look for her friends. Olivia couldn't wait to share her exciting news with them!

The girls were all over by the stage. Everyone was there except Andrea. *Where could she be?* wondered Olivia. Before she could ask the girls,

Made for each other

the mayor approached the microphone.

"Ladies and gentleman, closing out Night One of the World Petacular, please welcome to the stage . . . Andrea!"

The audience applauded as Andrea took the stage. She looked amazing in her sequined dress. She sat down at the piano and began to play. Andrea started singing and she sounded fabulous! She was a true superstar.

Everyone loved Andrea's performance. The crowd was dancing. It was a magical moment.

As the song ended, fireworks erupted over Heartlake City, making a beautiful reflection upon the glistening water. When Andrea sang the final note to her song, the crowd went wild with applause.

Andrea received a standing ovation and took a bow. Then, she motioned for all her friends to join her on stage so they could share the moment, too.

Andrea shines onstage

Together forever

The girls hugged in celebration—they had accomplished so much, but most important, they had done it together.